CW00968904

THE LUMBERJACK'S OBSESSION

A CURVY GIRL ALPHA MALE ROMANCE

ALPHA MALES LOVE CURVY GIRLS
BOOK TWO

KELSIE CALLOWAY

CONTENTS

1

WILLOW

I'm a sucker for weddings. There's just something about the joy and love in the air that captivates me completely. I cherish them so much that I decided to become a wedding planner, turning my passion into a profession. In fact, I love them so much that last year I was a part of five weddings, and this year I'm set to attend seven. Well, technically, eight if you count today's celebration.

Weddings are truly the most beautiful moment in a person's life — a tapestry of emotions woven together in a single day. I've walked down that aisle twelve times in the last two years, each time feeling the thrill of anticipation and the warmth of love enveloping the atmosphere.

Today, I have the incredible honor of doing it again for my best friend, Jessica. I've only ever been the bridesmaid, never the bride myself, but that doesn't diminish the magic of the experience. Each ceremony, with its unique charm and heartfelt vows, leaves an indelible mark on my heart, and I revel in the enchantment of it all.

The music fills the air, a melodic backdrop to the sea of smiling faces surrounding me, each person radiating joy and excitement. It's a beautiful sight, and I can't help but feel uplifted by the collective happiness. Sure, I often find myself squeezed into a dress that doesn't quite flatter my figure, and even though I've managed to catch the bouquet twice—*an ironic twist of fate*—I still find myself single, with no boyfriends in the last three years. Yet, despite it all, I remain a hopeless romantic, a true sucker for weddings.

"Willow, can you help me use the bathroom?" Jessica's voice cuts through my ruminations, and I turn to see her holding up the skirts of her stunning princess-style wedding dress. A wince crosses her face, revealing that she's clearly waited until the very last moment to ask for my assistance, and I can't help but chuckle at the urgency of her predicament. It's a familiar scene, one that adds a touch of humor to this otherwise magical day.

"Absolutely," I reply, a warm smile spreading across my face. "Anything for you, Jessie."

The closest I've ever come to experiencing my own wedding was three years ago when my last boyfriend and I ended our tumultuous relationship after two years of ups and downs. He had the audacity to claim that I wanted too much from him. To be fair, my request for monogamy came after I caught him cheating on me for the second time—a betrayal that stung deeply.

In a fit of rage, he stormed out, his parting words cutting like glass: if I paid more attention to how I looked and cared for my body, perhaps he wouldn't have felt the need to seek out women who he deemed physically attractive. His words still echo in my mind, a painful reminder of the insecurities that can linger long after love has faded.

That hurt a little bit. It stung, a sharp reminder of my vulnerability after everything I had been through. I strayed away from men and dating for a solid six months while I repaired my self-esteem, rebuilding the fragile pieces of my confidence as if they were a carefully crafted mosaic. Each day was a step toward healing, but there were moments when memories of him would creep in, and I'd find myself questioning whether I was worthy of love at all. Unfortunately, I still saw the prick around town occasionally, his smug smile igniting an anger within me that I had thought I'd left behind.

"You're a gem, Willow," Jessica announces with relief in her tone as she busies herself with washing her hands, the sound of water splashing a soothing backdrop to our conversation. "Thank you for everything you've done today. I'm sorry you couldn't meet the best man before today to practice for the rehearsal dinner or anything," she continues, her voice lightening the tension that lingers in the air. "But Stephen's best friend moved to Montana a few years ago, and even though the two of them stay in touch almost daily, Hawk wasn't able to get down here in time due to some snow on the roads."

I nod, appreciating her efforts to ease my mind. Yet, part of me couldn't help but wonder how this day would unfold, hoping it would be free from any reminders of the past that still haunted me.

I wave her off, trying to dispel her concerns. "You shouldn't be worried about that. Let me take care of things like that," I reassure her, my voice steady and calm. "Hawk and I will meet before the wedding, and we'll talk through everything we need to before we walk down the aisle. We'll have it all handled, I promise. You just focus on walking down the aisle and marrying the love of your life. That's your only job today, babe."

Jessica's eyes light up, and she breaks into a radiant smile, throwing her arms around my neck in a warm embrace. "I don't know what I would have done without you. You're the best." Her words wrap around me like a comforting blanket, and in that moment, I can feel the weight of the day's worries begin to lift.

Growing up, Jessica was always flitting from one boy to another, her laughter echoing in the hallways as she charmed her way through crush after crush. She continued that trend into college and afterward, effortlessly drawing attention wherever she went. I often thought she'd never settle down, her free spirit seemingly too wild for the confines of a committed relationship. But then, a year ago, everything changed when she met Stephen. It was love at first sight, a spark that ignited between them almost immediately. They both recognized that they were destined for something special, a happily ever after that others only dreamed about.

I remember the phone call vividly; it was a month into their relationship when she excitedly asked if I would start planning their wedding for them and if I'd be her maid of honor. At that point, he hadn't even proposed yet, but Jessica was certain it was only a matter of time. Three months later, she texted me with the date they had set, her excitement palpable even through the screen.

Even though I'm genuinely happy for Jessica, I can't shake the jealousy that gnaws at me from time to time. At twenty-eight years old, the most serious relationship I've had was with a man who left me because of my curves and a few extra pounds. He couldn't handle the way I filled out a pair of jeans, and even though the 'ass is back in' trend is all the rage now, he despised that I had one in the first place. So while Jessica is finding love effortlessly, without even looking for it, I'm left struggling to find a man who's interested enough to give me a second glance, let alone build a future with me.

I know that the right man is out there, waiting somewhere in the vast sea of possibilities. But sometimes, it's just downright depressing to think that I can't even manage to find a man, let alone the man who might make my heart race or feel like home.

"And you're sure he's the right one for me, Willow?" Jessica asks, her voice tinged with a mixture of excitement and apprehension as she pulls away from me, her fingers nervously chewing on her lower lip. It's a familiar sight—brides always seem to have this nervous energy coursing through them before the big day. Sometimes, it hits them weeks in advance, a fluttering anxiety that builds slowly, while other times, it strikes just minutes before they walk down the aisle, leaving them breathless and uncertain.

I reach for her hand, clasping it tightly in mine, hoping to convey the conviction I feel. "You're perfect for one another, Jessie. You both knew it the moment you met. I've had the privilege of watching the two of you blossom over this past year, and it's been an absolute joy to witness. Your connection is something truly special, and I can't wait to see what comes next for you both."

Her expression shifts slightly, and I can see the tension in her shoulders begin to ease. Jessica squeezes my hand in gratitude, a small smile breaking through her earlier uncertainty. "Okay, good. I was just worried. So many of my friends have had longer relationships and engagements than Jon and me. I started thinking that maybe we were rushing into this too soon, you know?" Her voice trails off, revealing the vulnerability she often hides beneath her bubbly exterior.

Having attended numerous weddings among our circle of friends, I had seen my fair share of couples who jumped into marriage far too quickly, even after spending five years together. It was disheartening to witness; they often lacked the essential communication skills needed to navigate the complexities of married life, or they simply didn't possess the tools to tackle the inevitable challenges that would arise. I learned that time alone doesn't determine the success of a marriage. It's really about the individuals involved and how well they complement and support each other.

"Don't worry, honey. I think you two will make it," I reassured her, my voice steady and warm. "Now go finish getting ready, and I'll see if I can catch up with Hawk for a bit."

2

WILLOW

The church that Jessica and Stephen have chosen looms before me, its vast structure both awe-inspiring and intimidating. It's practically a labyrinth of winding hallways that feed into one another, creating an intricate maze that feels like it could swallow me whole. As I round a corner, I suddenly find myself colliding with something solid and unyielding—a mountain, if you will. Or, more accurately, a mountain man.

"Excuse me, little lady," the mountain says, his voice deep and rumbling, infused with exaggerated politeness that feels almost comical in the moment, "I think I came at that corner a little too fast."

I apologize profusely, my cheeks flushing with embarrassment. "Wait, you must be Hawk!" A rush of recognition sweeps over me. I have known a majority of Jessica's friends since we grew up together, sharing countless memories and laughter, while Stephen's friends are a bit harder to pin down. However, I did manage to meet most of his inner circle at the rehearsal dinner last night, a whirlwind of introductions and polite chatter. Given that guests would be heading straight to the chapel, if this imposing man is wandering around where the bridal parties are changing, he must be one of them.

He tilts his head slightly, a playful glint in his eyes, and gives me a wide grin. "Does my reputation precede me?" His deep voice carries a hint of mischief, making me wonder just what stories have circulated about him.

Stephen mentioned he lived in the rugged mountains of Montana, showcasing his adventurous spirit, and he described himself as a muscular, fit, man's man, but he failed to mention that his best man was undeniably hot. "Sort of. I'm the maid of honor, Willow," I say, extending my hand to shake his, my heart racing at the unexpected chemistry crackling between us.

He takes my hand firmly in his and raises it to his lips, brushing them against my skin with a surprising gentleness. "Well aren't you the sweetest thing." Good God. Where did this sexy mountain fiend come from? His striking blue eyes twinkle down at me, framed by thick lashes, from his towering 6'5" frame, and when he finally releases my hand, there's a certain reluctance in his grip that leaves me momentarily breathless. "So tell me about yourself, Willow. What are you doing skulking about the hallways when the wedding is about to start in half an hour?" He leans in slightly as if genuinely interested, and I can't help but feel a flutter of excitement at the attention.

"Oh. Well, actually, I came to find you." The words tumble out of my mouth, and I can feel my cheeks warm as I trip over them.

Hawk glances around, scanning both directions as if ensuring we're alone. "Are we going to do this right now? Here? In the hallway?" He begins to roll up the sleeves of his suit with a teasing determination, revealing the toned forearms beneath. "You're gorgeous, Willow, and you're naughty. I suppose I'll risk getting caught for you," he adds, flashing me a wink that sends a thrill racing down my spine. The air between us crackles with anticipation, and I can hardly believe this moment is unfolding in the midst of all the wedding chaos.

Oh, dear. My cheeks flame a deep crimson, and my jaw drops open in disbelief. I'm utterly speechless, struggling to find the right words. "I-uh, well, um." I'm completely flabbergasted, caught off guard by his audacity.

Thankfully, he seems to take pity on my stammering.

"I was just joking," he says with that playful grin of his, the kind that makes my heart race. "I wouldn't take a beauty like you in the halls like this. Unless, of course, you were begging me for it." His cheeky wink sends another rush of heat to my cheeks, and I can't help but feel flustered all over again. "What can I help you with, Willow?" His tone is light, but there's an undercurrent of something more, something tantalizing, that keeps me hanging on his every word.

I clear my throat, trying to steady myself and return to the matter at hand before I completely turn into a pile of goo in front of him. "I just wanted to meet you and make sure that you knew what you were

THE LUMBERJACK'S OBSESSION

doing walking down the aisle. Jessica was worried since you weren't at the rehearsal dinner, and I told her I'd come to find you." As the words spill out, I can't help but wish I hadn't volunteered for this task, mostly because I'm beginning to doubt that this wave of embarrassment is going to dissipate before the wedding begins.

Hawk nods along as I speak, his arms crossed over his impressive chest. The sheer size of his muscles is striking, and for a fleeting moment, I find myself imagining that he might be one of the few men in the world capable of lifting me effortlessly. With his rugged beard framing his chiseled jaw and his slicked-back hair giving him that polished yet wild look, I don't doubt his mountain man schtick for a single second. "Well, I've walked before. Walking down the aisle is, what? A slower version of that? With a gorgeous woman on my arm? I think I can handle that." His voice carries a playful confidence that makes me bite my lip, torn between wanting to laugh and wanting to hide behind the nearest door.

If he doesn't stop calling me beautiful, he might have me begging for him to take me right here in these echoing hallways. "Well, good. Good, we talked then. I'll see you in a few minutes," I manage to reply, trying to sound nonchalant despite the way my heart races at the mere thought of him.

A smirk sits on his lips, as if he knows exactly the effect he has on me. "I can't wait," he says, his eyes sparkling with mischief and something deeper.

I turn around, but in my flustered state, I trip over my own two feet, stumbling forward like a clumsy fool. God damn it. What is this man doing to me? I catch myself just in time, but not before my cheeks flush with embarrassment. I can hardly believe I'm letting him have this effect on me.

3

HAWK

I think I'd rather be in Montana. I love Stephen; he's been my best friend since junior high, a constant in my life through all the ups and downs. But right now, this suit feels like a straightjacket, suffocating me with its stuffy fabric, too tight around every part of my body, and I can't shake the sensation that it's slowly choking me.

I almost didn't make it to the wedding. In my determination to ensure the guys watching my cattle were well informed about what needed to be done in my absence, I almost found myself caught in a blizzard yesterday. It was barely snowing when I first hit the road, but a couple of hours in, the storm intensified, and I couldn't see the lines on the road anymore. All I could do was keep my hands steady on the wheel, pressing forward and hoping for the best. I spotted cars abandoned on the side of the road, their drivers either having spun off or perhaps being wiser than I was, choosing to pull off and wait it out. But I had chains on the tires of my truck, and stubbornness coursed through me as I kept on going, determined to make it to the celebration, even if it meant facing the worst of the weather.

Thankfully, I made it without crashing. The good Lord saw fit that I should reach Stephen and Jessica's wedding, and I offered my gratitude for that small miracle.

Feeling the weight of the formal suit constricting me, I told Stephen I needed to get some fresh air before it tried to suffocate me. I stepped out of the groom's room, the air inside thick with anticipation and the scent of cologne, and made my way toward the exit. Just as I was about to push the door open, I collided with a beautiful woman in a hideous powder blue dress. She had to be one of the bridesmaids; no one in their right mind would willingly choose to wear that style and color for such a momentous occasion. The contrast of her striking features against the drab fabric was almost comical, and for a brief moment, I forgot about the suffocating suit as I took in her surprised expression.

I gave that gorgeous woman a once-over, my heart flipping over in my chest as if it had a mind of its own. A primal instinct surged through me, urging me to grab her by the waist, fling her over my shoulder, and whisk her away to my truck, where we could drive all night back to Montana under the vast, starry sky. But my brain chimed in, reminding me that I needed to lock her down before some other man swooped in and claimed her first. I glanced at her hands; there was no ring, no sign of commitment. That meant one of two things: either she had a clueless boyfriend who hadn't made a move yet, or she was single and ripe for the picking. In that case, I seriously considered moving away from Montana and heading down to Kansas, where I imagined the real women were, because good God, this woman was breathtakingly beautiful, and I couldn't let her slip away without at least trying to make a connection.

Then she introduced herself as the maid of honor, a title that carried a weight of significance since she would soon be walking down the aisle with me later today. In that moment, it felt as if the stars had aligned perfectly. God had genuinely whispered in my ear, "Hawk, don't freeze to death in the blizzard; you need to make it to this wedding and meet the woman of your dreams." And here I stood, utterly mesmerized before this curvy goddess, feeling an undeniable pull that made me ready and willing to consider spending the rest of my life with her.

Life has a funny way of weaving itself together, presenting you with everything you've ever longed for. When I made the decision to uproot my life and move to Montana, it was driven by the realization that Kansas couldn't offer me all that I desired. Sure, there were plenty of women back home, but the vast open spaces I craved were few and far between. I couldn't afford the land at a price that fit my budget, nor could I envision raising cattle or cultivating the lifestyle I had always dreamed about. Leaving behind the familiarity of everyone and everything I knew was a daunting task, a leap into the unknown, but it was a choice I had to make to carve out a better future for myself. It seemed now, in this pivotal moment, that the sacrifice was finally beginning to bear fruit.

Secluding myself in Montana was difficult, but it was undoubtedly worth every challenge I faced. The fresh air and breathtaking landscapes provided a backdrop that made the loneliness more bearable. As I settled into my new life, I made new friends and met a colorful array of people, each with their own stories to tell. I even ventured into dating a little, allowing myself to be open to the possibilities that lay ahead. I hired workers for my land, and as we toiled together under the vast sky, I found camaraderie in the shared sweat and laughter. Most of them became more than just colleagues; they transformed into friends, each one adding a unique thread to the fabric of my life. The days stretch long, filled with hard work and the satisfaction that comes from building something meaningful, but as I lay down to sleep each night, I am filled with a profound sense of peace, knowing that I'm finally living the life I've always dreamed of. Yet, despite the fulfillment I feel, there remains an emptiness— the love of my life, a couple of kids to share in this journey, and all the beautiful memories we'll make together along the way.

Then there's Willow. She might just be that woman I've been searching for. I don't know for certain yet, but she certainly looks the part, with her vibrant smile and sparkling eyes that seem to hold a world of warmth. When I joke with her, she blushes, and in that moment, she transforms into something even more adorable than before. The way she laughs, the way her cheeks flush with color, makes me wonder if she could be the missing piece to my puzzle. Each encounter with her feels charged with potential, and I can't help but hope that fate has a hand in bringing us together.

I wasn't sure if Stephen should have gotten married so quickly after meeting Jessica. The idea of love at first sight always sounded absurd to me, like a whimsical notion out of a fairy tale. But then I met Willow, and everything changed. Feeling that primal urge inside me rise up—an overwhelming desire that seemed to demand I run away with the maid of honor—I finally understood why he felt the need to lock his bride down so swiftly. I want nothing more than to make this stunning, curvy woman mine. I want to claim every part of her, to explore the depths of her laughter and the warmth of her smile.

As I watch her walk away, I can't help but chuckle when she trips over her own feet, a fleeting moment of clumsiness that only adds to her charm. I hope she is as affected by me as I am by her, as if the very air between us crackles with unspoken possibilities. My heart races at the thought, and I can't shake the feeling that our paths are meant to intertwine in ways I have yet to imagine.

4

WILLOW

"You're not going to trip again, are you?" Hawk whispers, his voice low and teasing as we stand side by side, our hearts racing with anticipation for the moment that lies ahead—walking down the aisle for Jessica and Stephen's wedding, a celebration of love and commitment.

I was really hoping he hadn't noticed my earlier stumble. "Are you going to catch me if I do?" I shoot back, my voice barely above a whisper, a playful challenge lacing my words.

"Of course," he replies, a smirk dancing on his lips, "but the only falling I want you to be doing is for me, Willow." His gaze holds mine, warm and inviting, and for a brief moment, the chaos of the wedding fades away, leaving just the two of us suspended in this shared moment filled with unspoken possibilities.

My heart flips over in my chest, and I can't help but steal a glance up at him. He gazes straight ahead, yet a confident smile lingers on his lips, hinting at mischief just beneath the surface. "Don't say things you don't mean," I retort, rolling my eyes, before turning my attention back to the scene unfolding before us as the music swells, enveloping us in its romantic embrace.

Hawk straightens his posture as if he's preparing for a grand performance. His already broad chest puffs out even further, the fabric of his suit jacket stretching against his pectorals, which seem to be practically bursting free. With a playful glint in his eye, he leans in slightly, his voice low and teasing. "I always mean what I say. Like when I say that I'd like to see what you look like without that dress on."

Before I have a chance to respond, he takes a confident step closer, closing the distance between us. With our arms linked together, my fate feels inextricably tied to his, as if he's weaving me into the very fabric of this moment. I paste a smile onto my face,

THE LUMBERJACK'S OBSESSION   29

desperate to mask the tumult of emotions swirling within me. A blush creeps back onto my cheeks, warm and undeniable, and I can't help but notice how my body betrays me; my panties are now damp with a longing that I haven't felt in years. It's both thrilling and terrifying, especially as I find myself thrust before a hundred and fifty of Jessica and Stephen's closest friends and family. I glance at him, hoping he's proud of himself for stirring this unexpected desire within me, even amid such a public spectacle.

As I step into the reception hall, the atmosphere buzzes with laughter and chatter, yet I feel a strange sense of solitude. I make my way to the head table, where I was originally seated next to Hawk at the end. Jessica had deemed it fitting for us to share the space, even though we weren't family, since we were both here to celebrate the union of the happy couple. But now, as I approach my seat, I find myself drawn toward a beaming Hawk, his smile bright and inviting.

"I think we walked down the aisle together quite beautifully," he announces with an easy confidence as I near him. His tone carries a playful lilt, and I can't help but feel a flutter of amusement at his suggestion. "We should try it again sometime soon." The way he says it makes the idea feel both light-hearted and enticing, and I can't shake the feeling that perhaps he's not just referring to the ceremony.

"Is 'forward' just your style of picking up women?" I ask as I settle into my chair, the warmth of the day still clinging to my skin. "Or do you just say whatever you think is going to make them blush?"

Hawk scoots his chair closer to mine, a playful glint in his eye. The reception hall is alive with laughter and chatter, the voices of guests overlapping like a symphony of celebration. I recognize many familiar faces milling about, but they all seem to respect this moment, choosing not to interrupt our conversation. Perhaps they think I'll look less engaged when the time is right, and they can swoop in for a chat.

"I just know a good thing when I see it," he replies, a confident smile spreading across his lips as he leans in slightly, as if sharing a secret that only we are privy to. The atmosphere around us feels charged, our playful banter weaving a bubble of intimacy amid the festive chaos.

I snort and shake my head, glancing around the room for the cocktail waiters who are supposed to be circulating with trays of wine. I could definitely use a glass—or three—right now to help wash away the sting of old memories. "According to my ex, you'd be wrong. Maybe if I lost thirty pounds, I'd finally be a good thing." I can hear the bitterness creep into my tone, sharp and unwelcome, and I wince at the sound of my own words.

"Honey, you're perfect just the way you are," he replies, his voice warm and reassuring. "I'm not sure what your ex said to you, but he was a damn fool. You're gorgeous. Perhaps not in that dress, but I think that was Jessica's way of making sure that none of you bridesmaids outshined her." Hawk shrugs with a casual confidence that makes me feel a little lighter. "Kind of hard to do that, though, because you're beautiful no matter what you wear." His words wrap around me like a comforting embrace, and for a moment, I forget the insecurities that have tangled themselves around my heart.

Who is this man? Should I really consider moving to Montana for a fresh start? "What's your deal, Hawk?" I turn to face him, my curiosity piqued and perhaps a little defensive. "Why do you keep calling me beautiful? I don't understand it. Did Stephen pay you or something?" I scan him from head to toe, a frown creasing my forehead as I try to make sense of his attention. "You could have your pick of any of the single ladies here, and yet you won't leave me alone. What's the deal?"

For a fleeting moment, I catch a glimpse of vulnerability in his expression, and my heart twinges with guilt. A frown crosses his usually jovial face, and I can see the hurt flicker in his eyes, almost as if I've wounded him with my words.

"Do you want me to leave you alone? Are you really not interested?" he asks, his voice tinged with a sincerity that makes me question my initial assumptions.

I scoff. "What?" He's the gorgeous one out of the two of us, after all. "Why wouldn't I be interested? You're sexy, Hawk. You have muscles on every conceivable surface, and the way you carry yourself exudes confidence. You reek of testosterone. Every single part of me just wants to rip off your shirt right now, and I barely even know you. This isn't who I am; I'm not usually this forward. But you, Hawk, you're a walking fantasy."

Hawk's smile returns, a radiant beam that lights up his handsome face, and I can see his spirits seem buoyed by my words. "I keep calling you beautiful because you are beautiful," he replies, his tone sincere. "You have curves in all the right places, Willow. I want to bury myself in you, but I'm a gentleman. I'd like to take you out on the dance floor first and spin you around, feel that connection between us. I want to share a glass of wine with you and let the evening unfold naturally. I want to tell you a story or two about Montana and what I do there, and I want to listen to some stories about your life—what makes you tick, what you dream about. Then, I want to suggest that we have a nightcap at your place or my hotel, wherever it feels right. And while we're laughing about one thing or another, I want to lean in and kiss you, taste that spark that's been lingering in the air between us. And as we take things further, I want to peel off that hideous dress that Jessica made you buy and see what lies beneath it, the real you that I know is waiting to be uncovered."

His words fan flames that I didn't even know existed, igniting a heat within me that feels both thrilling and terrifying. My breathing becomes erratic, each inhale shaky with a mix of anticipation and desire, and I bite my lip to keep myself from leaning forward and kissing him right then and there. He has this incredible talent for weaving an erotic scene, painting vivid images with nothing more than his voice. "And Stephen didn't pay you to say that, right?" I tease, trying to keep the mood light.

"Stephen still owes me $25 from fantasy football three years ago." He chuckles, and the sound sends delicious shivers down my spine.

I'm going to take that as a no. It's a slim possibility, but I've lowered the likelihood significantly. "Well, let's start with a glass of wine. If that goes well, we'll move on to those other things you mentioned," I suggest, my heart racing at the thought. Part of me desperately wants to skip to the end where he peels off the hideous dress that Jessica made me buy, revealing the real me that's been hidden beneath layers of fabric and expectation. But I remind myself that I'm a patient woman. What are a few hours of wining and dining before we get to the good stuff? Each moment spent in his company only deepens my yearning, making the promise of what's to come even more tantalizing.

5

HAWK

It doesn't surprise me at all that Willow has chosen to be a wedding planner. There's an undeniable sparkle in her eyes whenever she discusses anything related to weddings. She speaks about them with such passion and enthusiasm, as if they are the most glamorous and significant day of a person's life, a moment that deserves to be celebrated in all its glory.

"I know a lot of men aren't into the whole fairytale thing," she says, her smile wavering slightly, revealing a hint of vulnerability beneath her confident exterior. "But I genuinely enjoy making a person's dreams come true. Sure, it's just one day, but everyone remembers their wedding day. They might not recall all the little details, like the napkins or the flowers or whatever, but they will always remember the feeling of walking down the aisle and the joy of the reception. Those really big moments, you know? I'm sure this all sounds silly to you, considering you're the kind of person who does something so manly, someone who probably isn't into stuff like this." Her voice trails off, leaving a lingering curiosity about what she might think of me.

In some ways, she's right. I don't care about weddings as much as she does. The sheer fact that she's been in thirteen weddings in just two years is absolutely insane to me. "To be fair, my cattle aren't big on weddings. They just mate, and before I know it, it's calving season again. No fuss, no fanfare— just nature taking its course."

Her laughter bubbles up, and it's the most refreshing sound I've heard all day, brightening the atmosphere around us. "Well, how about you spin me around the dance floor for a song or two? I thought you said that was on the table, after all. You know, before you take off my dress." Her playful challenge hangs in the air, igniting a spark of excite-ment and mischief that I can't help but respond to.

Whether it's the wine talking or because she's finally coming around to see my side of things, I seize her hand before she has a chance to change her mind. "Your wish is my command, gorgeous."

As I guide her toward the dance floor, she lifts her free hand in a cheerful wave, greeting a few familiar faces scattered throughout the venue. "Hey, Sarah! Hi, Ben!" she calls out, each name rolling off her tongue effortlessly. Throughout the night, our conversation has been peppered with friendly interruptions, as several guests have stopped by to say hi, their curious glances darting between us. Each time, she's made it clear that I'm the best man, not just some random date. I can't help but feel a mix of pride and amusement at her insistence as if she's staking a claim to this moment we're sharing.

"So, at these twelve other weddings you've attended in the last two years, how many men did you dance with before me?" I ask, pulling her in close until she's pressed against my body. She fits like a glove; her curves align perfectly with mine, like a puzzle piece clicking into place, creating a warmth that radiates between us.

Her gaze drifts into the distance, a thoughtful expression crossing her face as if she's sifting through memories. "Maybe two? That's probably it. Nobody wants to dance with the fat girl, you know." Her voice carries a hint of vulnerability, and I can sense the weight of those past experiences lingering in her words. I wish I could erase those moments for her, to show her just how beautiful she truly is, especially in this moment where the music swells around us, wrapping us in its embrace.

"You're not fat." I pull her closer, wrapping my arms around her as we sway together to the rhythm of the music, feeling the soft vibrations reverberate through our bodies. "You're too hard on yourself, Willow. I really don't understand why you feel that way, either." I tilt my pelvis toward her, pressing gently into her lower belly, a palpable connection sparking between us. "Do you feel that? Do you feel my arousal? That's all for you, baby. Because you're absolutely gorgeous and incredibly sexy."

She lifts her gaze to meet mine, her eyes shimmering with a mix of vulnerability and desire, her breathing becoming slightly labored under the weight of her feelings. "Hawk," Willow whispers, her voice low and laced with longing. "You're too kind."

"I just say what I feel, honey. You're stunning beyond words." I lean down to kiss her softly, savoring the lingering taste of the sweet Moscato she had been sipping earlier. It's a flavor that dances on my tongue, mingling with the warmth radiating from her. As her tongue tepidly glides across my lower lip, a surge of electricity courses through me, and I can't help but smile into the kiss. She is the sweetest thing I've ever been with, and the desire to claim her in more ways than one swells within me like a tide.

Reluctantly, I pull away, my breath mingling with hers, creating a shared moment heavy with anticipation and unspoken words. "After the newlyweds leave, do you want to come back to my hotel?" I ask, my heart racing a little faster than I'd like to admit. "You can say no if you want; my feelings won't be hurt. Or if you say yes and decide later that you don't want to do anything, I understand that, too." The words tumble out in a rush, each one laced with sincerity. I want her to know, without a doubt, that she doesn't have to do anything she doesn't want to do. I want this to be about her comfort, her choices, and that reassurance hangs in the air between us, charged and waiting.

She seems a little hesitant, as though she's standing at the edge of a cliff, peering down into an unfamiliar abyss. It's as if she's navigating a territory she's never ventured into before, both thrilling and daunting. "I want you to feel comfortable, Willow. We can even go back to your place if you'd like. Or maybe I'll just give you my number and—"

But before I can finish my thought, she cuts me off, her voice firm yet tender. "Your hotel is perfect, Hawk. And if I want to stop, I'll let you know. But you have to know something." She glances down between us, a flicker of vulnerability in her eyes, before meeting my gaze again. I catch her chewing nervously on her lip, a small gesture that reveals the whirlwind of emotions she's grappling with. "I haven't done *it* before. There's just never been a right time or the right person. I wanted to," she says, her voice imbued with a mix of hope and trepidation, "but it just never happened for me. Is that... okay?"

It's more than okay. "Willow, I promise to take it slow with you. I want you to feel completely comfortable. And if you ever say stop, I'll stop—no questions asked. Whatever you want, honey, I'll be here for you."

She entrusts me with her most precious flower, and that's no small thing. It's a weighty responsibility, one that I don't take lightly. I can feel the gravity of the moment, a blend of excitement and seriousness swirling in the air between us. I'm ready for the challenge, eager to honor her trust and guide her gently into this new territory.

6

WILLOW

When we finally arrive at Hawk's hotel room, he greets me with an abundance of offers, everything from an array of sumptuous food and refreshing drinks to the promise of a deep tissue massage that sounds heavenly. I wish I could summon some nervousness, the kind of jittery anticipation that one might expect to feel before the first intimate encounter. But instead, a thrilling sense of excitement courses through me, igniting my senses.

Standing at the edge of a precipice, one is typically overwhelmed with anxiety about taking that fateful step off the ledge. Yet here I am, feeling an irresistible urge to leap headfirst into the unknown, ready to embrace whatever awaits me on the other side. The thrill of possibility wraps around me like a warm blanket, offering comfort in its own exhilarating way.

"What do you want to do first, Willow?" Hawk asks, his voice steady as he removes his suit jacket and hangs it neatly on the back of a chair, the crisp fabric contrasting with the warmth of the room.

I slip off my shoes, feeling the coolness of the floor beneath my bare feet, and he follows suit, his own shoes joining mine in a quiet pile. "I want you to take me. I want you to have your way with me as though I were any other woman. Forget what I said about being a virgin." The words tumble out, raw and unfiltered, as I search his eyes for understanding. I don't want him to feel nervous about having sex with me; I want to ease any tension that might linger between us. I'm sure I'll feel nervous enough for the both of us when it comes down to it, but I refuse to let that overshadow what I truly desire. "I want you to make me yours, Hawk." The weight of my confession hangs in the air, charged with the electricity of unspoken promise and anticipation.

A thrill courses through me as I feel his arousal, solid and unyielding, beneath his pants. "You have a way of bringing it out in me," I reply with a smirk, my heart pounding in my chest. He closes the distance between us, his hands firm on my hips as he pulls me towards him. My breath hitches as his lips meet mine, the kiss slow and deliberate, a promise of what's to come. His tongue teases mine, and a shudder runs down my spine, leaving me wet and aching for more. When he finally pulls away, I'm left gasping for breath, my body humming with desire.

I trace my fingers up his chest, feeling the firm muscles ripple beneath his shirt. It seems that working with cattle has its perks, I think wryly, as I begin to undo the buttons one by one. His skin is warm and inviting, and I can't help but let out a small sigh of pleasure as I explore the ridges and planes of his chest.

He pulls away from me suddenly, a mischievous glint in his eye. "Let's get you out of this dress," he says, his voice low and husky. I feel a thrill of antici-pation run through me as he turns me around and begins to undo the zipper on my dress. His hands are warm and strong on my back, and I lean into his touch as he slowly peels the dress away from my body. I can feel his breath hot on my neck as the dress falls to the ground, leaving me in nothing but my underwear. "God damn," he whispers from behind me, his voice filled with awe and desire. I can't help but smile at the compliment, feeling more confident and desirable than I have in a long time.

I turn to face him, letting him take in the full effect of the black, lace undergarments I slipped into this morning, the delicate fabric hugging my curves in just the right way. "What now?" I ask, my voice barely above a whisper, laced with a mix of curiosity and playful challenge.

His gaze intensifies, and I notice the way his breath catches slightly as he takes me in. "I'm going to need you to get on that bed," he says under his breath, his tone dropping an octave, thick with desire, as if the very air around us has ignited. The fire lighting up his eyes sends a thrill coursing through me. "Before I rip those panties off." His words hang in the air, charged with anticipation, and I can feel the tension between us crackling like electricity.

That sounds like a delectable treat, but given that this exquisite lace set cost me an arm and a leg, I can't help but comply with his orders. With a mix of anticipation and thrill fluttering in my stomach, I stride over to the bed, my heart racing with each step. As I crawl onto the soft covers, I take a moment to arrange the pillows just so, molding them to cradle my body until I find a position that feels both inviting and comfortable. The plush fabric beneath me whispers promises of indulgence, heightening the tension in the air as I settle in, awaiting his next move.

Hawk remains captivated, his gaze never wavering from me as he discards his shirt, revealing the taut muscles of his chest and abdomen. A shiver of excitement courses through me as he continues to undress, skillfully unbuckling his belt and sliding off his pants. The soft light in the room illuminates the contours of his body, casting enticing shadows that dance across his skin.

He shakes his head slightly, as if in disbelief, and murmurs, "You have no idea how alluring you are right now, Willow." The sincerity in his voice resonates deep within me, and I feel a blush spread across my cheeks. He takes a step closer to the bed, his eyes gleaming with admiration and desire. "I can hardly believe that I'm the one you've chosen to share this experience with. I'm truly humbled and grateful. And if I'm being completely honest, I think I've fallen in love with you, Willow."

I can't help but laugh, convinced that he's exaggerating for effect, but when I look at him, I realize he doesn't share in my amusement. His expression remains earnest and unwavering, leaving me to wonder if he's truly serious. Could he really mean what he says? The thought is both thrilling and bewildering, making my heart race in a way I didn't expect.

He prowls towards the bed with a predatory grace, his gaze riveted on my form. The intensity in his eyes is almost palpable, sending a shiver down my spine. "I should probably remove these," he murmurs, his voice low and husky as he hooks his thumbs into the waistband of his boxers. My breath catches in my throat as he slips them off, revealing his arousal in all its glory. The sight of him, so confident and unabashed, only serves to heighten my own desire. I feel my cheeks flush as I take in the full length of him, my heart pounding in anticipation of what's to come.

For a brief moment, I find myself lost in the absurdity of it all, wondering just how that impressive monster is meant to fit inside me. It seems almost surreal, like a fantastical creation that defies logic. Yet, somehow, everything about him appears to work in perfect harmony. The sheer size of him is both daunting and exhilarating, and I can't help but feel the urge to applaud this magnificent display of confidence and allure. My heart races at the thought, as if my body is already anticipating the impossible.

Hawk climbs onto the bed, a playful glint in his eyes, and begins his exploration with a soft kiss at my navel. "God, you're gorgeous," he murmurs, his voice low and filled with admiration. As he teasingly licks a circle around my belly button, a cascade of laughter escapes my lips, bubbling up from a deep well of delight. The sensation sends shivers down my spine, igniting a warmth that spreads through me, leaving me breathless and eager for more of his tender attention.

"Hey now," I chastise him, my voice light yet firm, "stop that. I'm ticklish."

He responds with a mischievous grin, the kind that promises trouble, and before I can react, he does it again, his playful fingers darting to my sides. He holds my hips firmly, ensuring I can't buck him away, his touch both teasing and possessive. "Laughter is great in the bedroom," he declares, his tone teasing, as I squirm and try to push him away, the sensation sending ripples of joy through me. "It's the sign of a great relationship." The warmth of his breath against my skin only adds to the fluttering butterflies in my stomach, making it hard to focus on anything but the delightful chaos he's created.

I slide further down on the bed, attempting to guide his attentions, and gratefully, his lips wander to my right hip. He showers it with kisses, nibbles, and licks, as if I'm a Willow-flavored ice cream cone and he's savoring every moment. The warmth of his touch spreads through me, and he's barely even begun to truly explore.

His hand drifts lower, finding its way to my pussy, where he teasingly traces the dampness he's instilled through the fabric. "Ah, it appears someone's more than ready," he murmurs against my skin, his voice a low rumble that sends shivers down my spine. "Perhaps it's time we remove these."

Though I know foreplay is meant to be a drawn-out affair, a part of me yearns for him to discard my panties and plunge into me without further delay. To cease the tantalizing preamble and claim me, body and soul.

He hooks his fingers into the waistband of my panties, the lace band a mere whisper against his skin as he begins to slowly draw them down. The pace is a deliberate tease, a sensual torment that makes me ache for more. My breath hitches as the cool air hits my exposed flesh, and I can't help but squirm beneath his gaze.

"Spread your legs, baby," he orders, his voice barely more than a growl. It's a command I can't refuse, a demand that sends a jolt of electricity through my body. I do as he says, opening myself up to him completely, my heart pounding in my chest.

He takes a singular finger and runs it across my slit, the sensation so powerful that I shudder, my body trembling with need. "You're so sensitive," Hawk announces, a note of satisfaction in his voice as he watches me react to his touch. I can only nod, my voice lost to the whirlwind of emotions that threaten to overwhelm me. I'm completely at his mercy, and I wouldn't have it any other way.

Then he dives back down to his previous position, but this time lower, kissing my thigh with an exquisite fervor, nibbling at the tender flesh that sends shivers coursing through me. Each teasing touch ignites a fire within, driving me up the wall with a mix of longing and desperation. I can hear my own sharp intake of breath, a sound laden with both surprise and pleasure, and his soft chuckle follows suit, rich and warm, sending ripples of excitement through the air that surrounds us.

He whispers tantalizingly, "I'm going to lavish my attention on your clit, darling, and once I've got you quivering with anticipation, I'll slip my fingers inside that sweet, welcoming warmth, readying your exquisite pussy for my throbbing cock." The promise in his voice is intoxicating, and I can barely contain my excitement. I manage a breathy, "Yes, please," as he adds, "But remember, if it ever becomes overwhelming, just tell me. Your pleasure is my utmost priority."

The sensations I'm already feeling are almost over-whelming, a delightful whirlwind of new experi-ences that send shivers of pleasure coursing through my body. Each touch ignites a spark within me, and I can hardly process it all. I feel like I'm teetering on the edge of sensory overload, lost in a haze of exhila-ration. The only response I can manage is a fervent nod, praying he understands the depths of what I'm experiencing. Yet, a man like him, so confident and skilled, has surely navigated this terrain more than a time or two. I can't help but trust that he knows exactly what he's doing, guiding me through this intoxicating journey.

Hawk's scorching mouth finds its way to my most sensitive spot, and I reflexively clutch the blankets as a rush of pleasure washes over me. His tongue plays a tantalizing rhythm, flicking back and forth over the swollen nub, sending jolts of electricity coursing through my body. I can barely contain myself as a solitary finger breaches my entrance, soon joined by another, both teasing and beckoning in a synchronized dance that has me arching my back, desperate for more. The sensation is almost too much to bear, yet I find myself craving the exquisite torment, my breath hitching as I surrender to his masterful touch.

With Hawk, the ascent to ecstasy is an exquisite journey unlike any I've experienced before. Vibrators have provided me with release in the past, and I'm no stranger to the sensation of an orgasm, but the way Hawk's mouth worships my most sensitive spot sets him apart. He applies the perfect amount of suction to my clit, eliciting moans that I can't contain as my hips instinctively rock in response. The relentless assault of his tongue – flicking, sucking, and circling – leaves me gasping for breath and calling out his name in a desperate plea for more.

Simultaneously, his fingers weave an intricate pattern within me, working in harmony with his skilled mouth to push me toward heights of pleasure I never imagined possible. Each deliberate stroke and teasing caress from his fingers sends waves of euphoria crashing over me, leaving me completely at his mercy. The combination of his talented tongue and the synchronized movements of his fingers is a potent cocktail that has me teetering on the edge of release, craving the sweet oblivion that only Hawk can provide.

When the orgasm rips through me, it catches me off guard, leaving me utterly unraveled. I cry out Hawk's name as if it's my last lifeline, my voice echoing through the room as I shatter into a thousand shimmering fragments. Yet, even as the intensity peaks, he doesn't relent. His masterful tongue continues its relentless exploration, while his fingers persist in their intimate dance, massaging my most sensitive spots with unyielding precision. It's as if he instinctively understands that I need this prolonged stimulation to fully experience the exquisite ripples of my release. As the waves of pleasure finally begin to subside, I lay there, utterly spent and completely enthralled by his skillful touch.

"You taste like honey, honey," he says, his voice a sultry whisper that sends shivers down my spine as I finish, my body glistening with a thin layer of sweat that catches the light like tiny diamonds. "I knew when I kissed you earlier that you were the sweetest thing I'd ever had. This only confirms that. Like cantaloupe juice, so rich and intoxicating."

I glance down, my breath hitching in my throat as I see his face pop up between my thighs, a playful glint in his eyes. "How did you do that?" I ask, genuinely astonished, a mix of disbelief and wonder threading through my voice.

He simply shrugs, a nonchalant gesture that belies the proud smile that dances on his lips, a smile that radiates confidence and satisfaction. "Want me to do it again?" he teases, his tone both inviting and mischievous, as if he knows exactly the effect his words have on me.

7

WILLOW

As I try to collect my thoughts, I can't help but marvel at the man before me. How did I manage to find someone who sees me as beautiful and desirable, and who takes such pleasure in giving me earth-shattering orgasms? It feels like a dream, a fairytale come to life. But is this what fairytales are truly made of? As my mind races with questions, I realize that this doesn't feel real. It's too good to be true.

"I want more, Hawk," I whisper, my voice barely audible. "What you just did was incredible, truly amazing. But I know there's more to sex than just that. I want you to have me in other ways, to explore my body and discover all the secret pleasure spots that I've been longing to share with someone."

My heart races as I wait for his response, hoping that he'll understand what I'm trying to say. I want to experience the full range of what sex has to offer, to push beyond my comfort zone, and discover new heights of pleasure. And I want to do it with Hawk, the man who has already shown me that he's capable of making me feel things I never thought possible.

"That's what I like to hear, baby," he says, his voice dripping with confidence as a smirk dances across his lips. "How fast can that bra come off?"

With a rush of exhilaration, I sit up, feeling the weight of his gaze on me as I reach behind my back. My fingers fumble for a moment with the hook and eyelet, a mix of nerves and excitement coursing through me. I finally manage to unfasten it, and with a teasing grin, I let it fall, watching it flutter to the floor beside the bed like a forgotten memory. "That quick," I reply, my heart racing as I revel in the thrill of the moment.

His gaze devours me with an intensity that sends shivers down my spine. I've never seen a man look at me quite like this, with such raw appetite and desire. It feels as though he wants to consume me whole, enveloping me in his fervor. "You're a goddess," he whispers, his voice low and reverent, as he crawls the rest of the way up the bed, his movements deliberate and enticing. With each inch he gains, he pushes me down, and I can't help but feel both vulnerable and powerful at the same time. "You deserve to be worshipped," he adds, and the weight of his words wraps around me like a warm embrace, igniting something deep within.

As his mouth descends on my nipple, I feel a shiver of pleasure run down my spine. His tongue flicks my sensitive bud with an expertise that takes my breath away, mimicking the way it teased my clit just moments before. The sensation is wet and hot, and I find myself squirming with wanton desire beneath him.

Hawk's cock presses against my thigh, a thick and heavy reminder of what's to come. I can't help but wonder how it's all going to fit, but the anticipation only adds to my excitement. I know he has something amazing in store for me, and I can't wait to experience it. The weight of his body on top of me is both comforting and exhilarating, and I feel myself giving in to the moment completely.

"You're more than ready," he whispers against my breast, his hand sliding down between my legs to palm my slick folds. The sensation of his calloused fingers against my sensitive skin sends a jolt of pleasure through my body.

I've never wanted anything more than I want him in this moment. "Yes," I breathe, trying to keep my voice steady as desire threatens to overwhelm me.

He guides his thick cock to my entrance, teasing me with the tip as he presses against my wetness. I can feel myself stretching to accommodate him, and I savor the delicious ache that comes with it. He takes his time, entering me inch by slow inch, and I appreciate the care he's taking with me.

When he finally stills, fully seated inside me, he stops playing with my nipple and looks me in the eye. The intensity of his gaze sends a shiver down my spine, and I can see the desire mirrored in his own eyes. He wants this just as much as I do.

With a gentle thrust, he begins to move inside me, and I feel myself surrendering completely to the moment. The weight of his body on top of me, the feel of him filling me up, it's all more than I ever could have imagined. And I know that this is just the beginning.

As I adjust to his size, I can feel myself stretching to accommodate him, every nerve ending in my body heightened and sensitive to his touch. I dig my fingers into the firm muscles of his forearms, using them as an anchor to steady myself as he continues to push deeper. With each new inch, I gasp and bite my lip, trying to contain the overwhelming sensation of being completely filled by him. It's almost too much, but at the same time, it's exactly what I've been craving. I can feel my body yielding to his, surrendering completely to the pleasure of our connection.

"How does it feel, Willow?" He whispers in my ear, his breath hot against my skin.

His pelvis is pressed firmly against mine, and I know that I've fully accommodated his massive length and girth. I feel a sense of fullness that is both comforting and exhilarating. I could live in this moment forever, lost in the sensation of being completely connected to him. "I like this," I say with a shy smile, my voice barely above a whisper. "What else does it do?"

Hawk chuckles softly, the sound sending a shiver down my spine. "Remember that orgasm from before? It does something like that." He draws his hips back ever so slightly, allowing me to adjust to the new sensation before he begins to thrust in and out. Each stroke is slow and deliberate as if he is savoring the feeling of being inside me. I moan with excitement as he begins to pick up speed, his thrusts hitting a spot deep inside that feels new and unexplored. It's a different kind of pleasure than I've ever experienced before, and I can feel myself getting lost in the sensation. I dig my fingers into his firm forearms, using them as an anchor to steady myself as he continues to move inside me. With each new stroke, I can feel my body yielding to his, surrendering completely to the overwhelming pleasure of our connection.

Heeding his command, I obediently wrap my legs around his waist, pulling him further into me. The sensation of his manhood is indescribable, surpassing anything my vibrator could ever offer. Each stroke feels like a new discovery, an uncharted territory that leaves me breathless and yearning for more.

As I tighten my grip around him, he delves deeper still, striking that elusive spot with even greater precision. The pleasure intensifies, sending shockwaves through my body and pushing me to the brink. "Harder," I beg, my voice barely a whisper as I struggle to maintain my composure. I know that if he maintains this pace, if he continues to hit that sweet spot with just the right amount of force, I'll be sent soaring into ecstasy. I can feel it building within me, an unstoppable wave that threatens to consume me entirely.

With that, Hawk seems to need no further prompting. He leans in closer, his lips finding the sensitive spot at the base of my neck. He nips and bites at the tender flesh there, sending shivers down my spine as his thrusts grow more forceful. The exquisite mix of pain and pleasure from his bites and the feel of his cock hitting that perfect spot inside me is almost too much to bear. I clutch at his arm, my fingers digging into his skin as I fight to maintain some semblance of control. I can't help but scream out his name as I arch my back, meeting him thrust for thrust as an intense orgasm washes over me.

Hawk follows soon after, a deep, guttural grunt escaping his lips as he releases inside of me. I can feel the warmth of his seed filling me up, and I'm grateful for the small mercy of birth control. As we both come down from our high, I can't help but feel a sense of satisfaction and contentment wash over me. It's moments like these that make it all worth it.

I can feel the weight of his head against my chest, heavy and satisfied as he finishes, pumping the last of himself out with each final thrust. His breathing is ragged, matching my own as we both try to catch our breath.

Hawk swears under his breath, a low "Fuck me," that makes me smile despite myself. He rolls over to the side of me, his body still slick with sweat. I can feel the absence of him already, a sudden emptiness that makes me want to pull him back.

But he's already propping himself up on one elbow, looking down at me with a smirk. "So," he says, his voice low and husky, "how was your first time, gorgeous?"

I can feel the blush creeping up my cheeks, but I don't try to hide it. "It was...amazing," I say, my voice barely above a whisper. "I never knew it could feel like that."

Hawk's smirk turns into a full-blown grin, and he leans down to press a soft kiss to my lips. "I'm glad," he says, his breath warm against my skin. "I'm glad I could be the one to show you."

8

HAWK

As I gaze at Willow, the faint lines around her eyes and the slight droop of her shoulders reveal the exhaustion she's trying to hide. Yet, her radiant smile and the sparkle in her eyes tell a different story. A story of contentment and gratification.

"I couldn't have asked for a better first time," she murmurs, her voice barely above a whisper. Disbelief tinges her words as she shakes her head, causing her chestnut curls to sway gently. "Two orgasms?" she repeats, as if still trying to wrap her mind around the idea. "I wasn't even expecting one, let alone two." She lets out a soft chuckle, her cheeks flushing with embarrassment and delight. The sight of her happiness fills me with a warmth that spreads through my chest, making my heart swell with affection.

I find myself reflecting on the women I've shared my life with throughout the years, and nothing even begins to compare to my time with Willow. Sure, she may not have taken the lead in our encounter, but there's an exciting world of possibilities ahead of us. We have all the time in the world to explore each other's desires, to learn the tricks that will enhance our connection. I can show her the ways to bring me pleasure, and in return, I can discover the little things that ignite her passion. Tonight, however, was all about her, her joy, her satisfaction.

As Willow rises to use the restroom and tidy up, I can't help but watch her graceful figure move away from me. The sight of my essence glistening on her thighs fills me with an unexpected sense of pride and masculinity. It's a strange but exhilarating feeling, knowing that I've left my mark on her. I realize I should have asked for her consent before letting go, but in the heat of the moment, everything had felt so right. While I know I ought to apologize for my impulsiveness, my thoughts shift dramatically when she emerges from the bathroom, her skin glowing and fresh from a quick shower. The way she looks, radiant and revitalized, sparks another idea within me, one that promises to deepen our connection even further.

"Do you trust me?" I ask as she glides back onto the bed, the way her body moves captivating my attention.

Her eyes narrow slightly, a mixture of playfulness and hesitation flickering across her features, and a reluctant smile curls at the corners of her lips. "Maybe. Why?"

I take a breath, feeling the weight of the moment, the air thick with anticipation. "I want you to sit on my face. I want to give you a third orgasm." The words hang in the air, charged with an electric intensity, a promise of pleasure that dances between us.

Willow's cheeks bloom a vivid crimson once more, reminiscent of earlier today when I playfully teased her about the possibility of taking her in the hallway of the church. "Hawk, I can't do that. I'll suffocate you. I'll crush you to death. I'll—"

I interrupt her, unable to let her spiral into such absurdity. "You're not going to do anything of the sort. Now, get that gorgeous ass up here," I command, gesturing toward my face, "because I want to have you this way." The weight of my desire hangs between us, making the air thick with tension and anticipation.

I can see the internal struggle playing out on Willow's face, but eventually, she seems to come to a decision. With a hint of reluctance, she positions herself over me and starts making her way up my body. I can feel the heat radiating off of her as she moves closer.

"If you can't breathe, just double-tap my thigh or something," she says, still sounding uncertain. "I'd feel terrible if I ended up being responsible for the death of the man who took my virginity."

I can't help but grin up at her. "If this is how I go, then I'll die as the luckiest and happiest man in the entire universe," I reassure her. The anticipation building between us is electric, and I can't wait to feel her above me.

I eagerly grab her hips, guiding her into position above me. Her wetness brushes against my lips, sending a jolt of pleasure through my body. I can't help but groan in anticipation as I prepare to taste her.

With a sense of urgency, I dive into exploring her folds with my tongue. I lick and suck at her sweet spot, savoring the taste of her arousal. Her thighs tighten around my head, creating a cocoon of warmth and intimacy. I feel a deep sense of satisfaction knowing that I'm the one bringing her pleasure.

Willow's grip on the headboard tightens as the sensations become too much for her to bear. I can hear her moans turn into cries of pleasure as my tongue swirls around her clit. The sound of her taking the Lord's name in vain only spurs me on, and I continue to tease and play with her until she's panting and gasping for breath.

In this moment, I feel truly alive and connected to her in a way that I've never experienced before. I could stay here, with my face buried between her thighs, for hours on end, worshiping her body and bringing her to the brink of ecstasy over and over again.

Exploring new territory, I gently trace one of my fingers along the edge of her other entrance. I'm not an expert in this area, but curiosity drives me to test the waters. The moment my finger grazes her hole, she reacts with a gasp of pure delight, and I can't help but grin against her slick folds. It seems she's open to this new sensation.

As I feel her grinding more insistently against my face, I sense her approaching climax. I adjust my technique, alternating between licking, sucking, and twirling my tongue in a relentless rhythm. Soon, her hips are rocking furiously against my mouth, and she's riding my face with the fervor of a creature in heat. When her release finally crashes over her, her sweet juices coat my beard, leaving me in awe of her breathtaking beauty.

"Oh god, Hawk, I have to lie down," she gasps, her legs quivering with the aftershocks of her pleasure, "I can't hold myself up here anymore."

Her breathless urgency ignites a spark of concern within me, though I know she's utterly spent. She never needed to worry about balancing herself; the sheer intensity of the moment had taken its toll. "Do whatever you'd like, babe," I say softly, my voice low and reassuring as I carefully help her off, cradling her gently in my arms to ensure she feels safe and supported. The warmth of her skin against me lingers, a reminder of the exhilarating connection we've just shared.

"You're too good to me," Willow bemoans as she lays down on the pillow, her voice taking on a sleepy, dreamy tone. The third orgasm must have done a number on her, leaving her in a blissful haze, her eyelids fluttering like delicate butterfly wings.

I lean over to kiss her gently on the forehead, cherishing the softness of her skin and the warmth radiating from her body. Some women don't like having their own juices in their mouth, so out of respect, I refrain from kissing her on the lips, even though the desire is strong. "I was lucky to find you, gorgeous," I whisper, my voice low and full of sincerity. "I hope I never lose you. In fact, I'm really hoping you'll come back with me to Montana. Or, at the very least, consider dating me." The words hang in the air between us, infused with hope and longing, as I watch her slowly succumb to the drowsiness that envelops her like a soft blanket.

She looks at me through sleepy, satiated eyes, a soft smile playing at the corners of her lips. "You know, I never thought that when I found the man of my dreams, it would be love at first sight. I thought he'd have to overlook how I looked." Her voice is a gentle murmur, a sweet confession that lingers in the air.

"Looking at you is my favorite thing. You're perfect, Willow." I can't help but mean every word. The way her hair spills across the pillow, the way the moonlight dances on her skin—it all makes my heart swell.

She snuggles closer to me, her warmth radiating against my side. "I love it when you say that. It makes me feel, I don't know, like maybe you're the person for me." The sincerity in her tone sends a rush of warmth through me, a thrill that ignites my hope.

I hold her tightly, feeling her heartbeat synchronize with mine as I let her drift off to sleep in my arms, her breathing becoming slow and rhythmic. "I hope I am the person for you. Because I can't imagine that there's anyone else out there for me." The words slip from my lips like a prayer, a silent vow that fills the intimate space between us. I don't know if she hears it, but I'll be right here when she wakes up to say it again, ready to remind her just how much she means to me.

ALSO BY KELSIE CALLOWAY

For more books...

Check out my Amazon page:

https://geni.us/KelsieCallowayAmz

Check out my website:

https://geni.us/KelsieCalloway

HAVE YOU LEFT A REVIEW?

Reviews are an author's bread and butter. This is how new readers find us and how old readers determine if a new series is worth their time. If you enjoyed this book, take a moment to leave a review or put in a recommendation on BookBub.

GET A FREE KELSIE CALLOWAY BOOK!

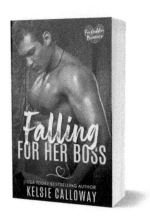

Join my mailing list to be the first to know about new releases, book sales, free promos, bonus content, and other author giveaways.

Get **Falling For Her Boss** free when you sign up!

Scan with your phone camera!

Milton Keynes UK
Ingram Content Group UK Ltd.
UKHW040306181024
449757UK00005B/354